Underground Aliens

A Story of Hollow Earth

Written by
April Christine Slocum-Alzhrani

Illustrations by
Alfin Fadholi

UNDERGROUND ALIENS - A Story of Hollow Earth

Copyright © 2021 by April Christine Slocum-Alzhrani

Illustrations and book cover by Alfin Fadholi

First printing in hardcover, paperback, ebook, and audio book editions May 2021

ISBN 978-1-7774622-4-6 Paperback Book

ISBN 978-1-7774622-6-0 Hardcover Book

ISBN 978-1-7774622-5-3 Electronic Book

ISBN 978-1-7774622-7-7 Audiobook

www.sailorslocum.com

http://youtube.com/sailorslocum

Write to the author: sailor.slocum@protonmail.com

Dedication

This book is dedicated to my daughters Elizabeth Anntoinette, Virginia Rayleen, Breanna Esther, and my grandchildren Millicent, Jude, Jericho, and Juno.

"We are with those we love; to live peacefully inside the village of the people we have created is our greatest joy and the fabric of all human health and unity in this physical world."

-April Christine Slocum

It was a dark and cloudy day with blustering icy winds. The Antarctic seemed to be a world of its own, apart from Earth itself. Milicent and her little brother Jude huddled quietly underneath a worn old blanket used to cover cargo in their grandfather's military plane.

They had quietly stowed away on board his flight to the mysterious bottom of the world: the Antarctic. They had heard their grandfather tell of a huge secret entrance to the center of the Earth and how he had seen many shimmering silver airships flying at high speeds in and out of its core. They knew that this particular flight was going to be Grandfather's plunge into an exploration of that mysterious hole in the Earth. They knew that Grandfather would never agree to take them on such a dangerous adventure and that they were not allowed to be inside the military plane, so they had carefully planned their secret stowaway, and it had worked until now...

"Ooohhhh," groaned Jude. "I need to use the bathroom! My tummy hurts," he cried.

It had been a seven-hour flight, and the two children had managed to stay quiet and unnoticed by their grandfather until now.

"What's this?! Who's there?!" called Grandfather, with surprise.

The children slowly pulled the blanket down from around their heads and faces. They looked out at their grandfather with shame and guilt-filled eyes.

"We are sorry, Grandfather," cried Milicent with a frown.

"We really wanted to come on this adventure with you and see the shining ships and the secret world underneath the ice. Please forgive us for not asking permission and for sneaking onboard," she pleaded.

But before Grandfather was able to say another word, the plane suddenly jolted and began to head down towards the ice. Grandfather pulled up on the throttle as hard as he could and started pushing buttons to try and regain control of the plane. An invisible force had gripped the plane and was pulling it into a giant dark hole in the ice.

"What's happening?! Are we headed into the center of the Earth?!" Jude exclaimed as he ran to the front of the plane.

Milicent closed her eyes and grabbed onto the furry stowaway hiding quietly underneath the blanket. She and her brother had brought their beloved dog Muffin along for the adventure.

"Woof woof!" barked Muffin; she was happy to be out from under the blanket.

"Oh no!" exclaimed Grandfather, "you brought the dog with you too?!"

"Don't worry, Grandfather!" said Jude, "Muffin can help us find our way out from the center of the Earth if we get lost, and also help scare away any aliens that may not be friendly."

Grandfather was speechless and just stared with his mouth open.

The engine began to make a loud humming sound as it fought against the force that was pulling the plane towards the Earth. Everyone had to cover their ears and Muffin began to HOWL. Then all of a sudden, everything stopped!

The plane just seemed to float in silent darkness within an inner space. Jude and Milicent tried to speak but no sound left their mouths. They could see their dog barking but they could not hear a sound.

Suddenly, they were no longer inside the airplane and they found themselves standing on a platform levitating above a new and unusual world. They could see a large pyramid shining in the distance, and there seemed to be land and an ocean that stretched out as far as the eye could see. Near the pyramid, the children and Grandfather noticed a large field covered in giant flying ships of different shapes and sizes. The ships hovered above the ground without a sound. Grandfather, Milicent, and Jude were amazed by the vastness of this new world inside the Earth.

"HELLO," echoed a voice. "You should not have come here; now the Galactic Federation will need to decide what will be done about your presence here."

The voice sounded concerned but gentle. Grandfather gathered the children and Muffin close to him.

"Show yourself," ordered Grandfather. "These children have been brought here by accident. I need to take them home. They have a mother up above who will be very worried about them being gone for so long."

A woman dressed in white robes with crystal clear hair and the palest skin materialized before them. Her piercing blue eyes seemed to see right into their souls as she spoke.

"This is not the world for your kind. There are many beings here that will be a danger to you if they find you here. You must come with me now; I will take you to a different part of this world where you will be much safer. There we will meet with the Federation to plan what will be done with you."

Suddenly, just as soon as she had finished speaking, they found themselves on the ground surrounded by fig trees and date palms. The weather felt warm and the sun shone down on their faces. They could still see the pyramids in the distance and the field of hovering airships.

Among the fig trees and palms they saw a group of aliens; some sat on large white stones, eating bowls of colorful fruits, and some walked slowly around, enjoying each other's company.

The lady announced their presence, and all the aliens gathered into a circle around Grandfather and the children.

"Why have you come here? " asked a tall thin gray alien with large dark eyes.

"I came to investigate what is happening inside our planet," replied Grandfather. "The people on the surface are sensing that something is wrong with life above. There is much confusion and sadness on Earth. It was not my plan to bring the children and the dog with me."

The beings of the Federation looked at each other and then back at the family without speaking aloud. They seemed to be talking to each other within their own minds, and Grandfather and the children could not hear what they were saying.

After a while, the lady took Grandfather and the children to wait in a holding dome. It was clear like glass but it had no door.

"No way to get out!" cried Milicent.

"Grandfather, are we going to be able to go home soon?" Jude asked. Muffin began to whimper. Everyone had become worried. They decided to sit down and wait quietly. As they sat waiting, they heard an announcement that seemed to ring inside their heads.

A voice shouted, "All Super Soldiers, to your ships at once! It is time to go above and practice our plan to frighten the population of humans and to take full control of them. Have the humans believe they are being attacked by aliens from distant planets so that we can create fear and war amongst them!"

Grandfather and the children very quickly became even more worried, but they did not know what to do.

A few minutes later, they heard a strange scratching noise and dirt began to fly through the air, and some even hit Jude in the face.

"Ouch!" cried Jude. "What is going on?!"

"LOOK!" cried Milicent. "Muffin is digging a way out underneath the dome!"

"Good dog!" cheered Grandfather, smiling. "Let's help her dig. We need to get back to our plane as fast as we can and get out of here. We need to warn the world about this terrible Super Soldier plan."

The children, Grandfather, and Muffin dug as fast as they could until they had made a very nice sized tunnel to crawl through.

"Look over there!" exclaimed Jude. It's grandfather's airplane, behind those spaceships."

"Let's make a run for the plane, kids. Be careful not to be noticed because we do not know what they will do if they catch us here," said Grandfather. "Ready... set... go!"

Everyone took a deep breath and started running towards the field of spaceships.

As they ran, they could see the silver spaceships were being guarded by superhuman soldiers and a tall grey alien with big black eyes. They overheard a human soldier talking to another human soldier about a mission they had just come back from.

"Our troops have completed the chemtrails above the Earth's outer crust. The sun will soon be blocked out. The Earth will become dark and cold," reported the soldier.

"Excellent!" exclaimed the other soldier. "The plan is falling into place."

Grandfather and the kids hid quietly behind one of the ships as they listened to the evil plot to destroy and enslave humanity on the surface.

"Oh no!" whispered Milicent, "What shall we do? How can we stop them?

"We will think of something," replied Grandfather.

Suddenly, a loud siren started to blare, and a loud voice announced, "Intruders at ship number 6... seize them!"

The family was instantly surrounded by a group of superhuman military men and then taken inside the large pyramid. A giant alien with white skin, long red hair, and a beard appeared before them. He was angry and ordered the soldiers to take them down to an area below the pyramid.

There, Grandfather and the kids saw scientists creating unusual plants and strange-looking animals; some looked like they were half-bird and half-lion, and some looked half-human and half-crocodile. It was very hot and they could hear moaning and crying out in the dark shadows surrounding them. Nobody spoke a word as they were led down through tunnels and through rooms made of rock. It became darker, and suddenly, they were standing alone in a cave beneath the ground that was surrounded by molten rock, smoke, and fire.

"Where is Muffin?!" cried Milicent. "She must have gotten lost!" She began to cry.

Grandfather and Jude looked worried and began calling for their dog.

"Muffin, Muffin, here girl!" they shouted. But not a sound was heard... no barking, no Muffin.

There seemed to be many dark shadows that faded in and out and moved quickly in a circle around them. Jude and Milicent rubbed their eyes.

"Are we seeing things? I don't like this place, it makes me feel heavy and sad inside," said Milicent.

"Yes, I feel it too," said Grandfather. "This is a bad place and we need to find a way out of here."

Then Jude had an idea.

"Grandfather," he whispered. "What if we hold hands and use our minds and words to call out to the nice lady who helped us when we first arrived; maybe she will hear us even from down here."

"Excellent idea, Jude," said Grandfather. "Let's try it."

Everyone held hands, closed their eyes, and bowed their heads to concentrate on calling up to the lady for help.

Within moments, they saw three circles of light heading toward them. The circles of light turned into the lady, and a man with gentle eyes and long dark hair, and with them was their dog Muffin.

The lady spoke. "This is why I asked you to listen to my words. I was trying to protect you from the evil ones. I could not come to this place alone to fetch you. The king of our people agreed to come with me to save you," she said.

"Oh thank you, thank you," the children cried. "And thank you so much for finding and bringing Muffin back to us! We were so worried about her."

"It was Muffin that came to us," the lady replied. "Almost all animals are pure of heart and can easily call out to the beings of our kind. Muffin knew you were in danger."

"Now come," said the king, "we will leave here. I will take you back to your plane and I will see that you make it back out into the sky. Remember what you have experienced here, and warn all who will listen above on the Earth. Tell them to make their hearts pure, to fight against the evil ones."

The king looked sad as he began to speak again. "There will be many who will not believe your words and many who will be cruel to you and put you through great hardship as you spread your message. Remember to be brave and true, and that I will always be near. Remember me and I will remember you.

As soon as the king had finished speaking, they found themselves inside their plane.

The engine turned on by itself and the plane was lifted up and began to move towards the entrance in the ice above.

Grandfather was relieved that they were on their way out of the center of the Earth, but his mind suddenly began to wonder what he could tell humanity about the experience, and how he would help people prepare for the evil that hid underground.

Then the voice of the king seemed to echo through the plane and into their heads: "Tell all who will hear you to be truthful and just, and to care for each other with generosity and kindness. Gather and store food, locate groundwater, never deceive others, and never follow what an evil being tells you, no matter how afraid you may be. Avoid anything that is impure, and respect the land, water, air, and animals of the Earth." As the king spoke, a peacefulness surrounded Grandfather and the children.

Then the king spoke once more. "I am the one who will return to help give all humans with loving hearts and good intentions a beautiful new world."

The plane suddenly started moving very fast and they were once again plunged into darkness. Muffin tried to bark but no sound came out of her throat. Milicent and Jude huddled together with Muffin underneath the old grey blanket.

Then in a flash of light, they found themselves back in the sky, flying over the icy Antarctic.

"We will be back home in a few hours, kids," Grandfather sighed.

Everyone was silent on the trip home because they had much to think about and do when they got back home.

After several hours, the sun began to set, and Grandfather landed the plane at the Air Force base. The children, Muffin, and Grandfather all walked off the plane and expected people at the base to be asking them questions... but nobody seemed to notice them or even care that they were there.

"That's odd," said Grandfather. "We have been gone for at least five days without any word, so I would have thought there would be people searching for us and maybe even a news crew here when we landed. But nobody seems to realize we were gone."

"Maybe we should go home to see Mother. She will have noticed we were missing, and she must be very worried," said Jude.

"Yes," said Grandfather, "we will head straight home right now."

As soon as the children arrived home, they ran through the door as fast as they could, with Muffin and Grandfather right behind them.

"Mother! Mother!" Milicent and Jude cried. "We are back! We are OK, don't worry!"

"What is all this yelling about?" asked Mother, looking puzzled. Go wash up for dinner now, I have already set the table."

Grandfather, Muffin, and the children stared at mother with their mouths open in surprise.

"But Mother," cried Jude, "we have been gone for days! Didn't you notice?! Didn't you miss us?! Weren't you worried?!

"Don't be silly," stated Mother. "Are you playing a joke on me? You both went outside to play with Muffin in the backyard not 15 minutes ago, and your Grandfather was headed out to the base. I'm glad he changed his mind about having dinner before going on a plane trip."

Grandfather and the children just stood there and looked at each other in amazement. Somehow, when they had been sent back out of the center of the Earth, time had gone backward and they were put back to the exact time that they had left.

After they had finished dinner and had their bath, Grandfather tucked the children into bed.

"Tomorrow," he said, "we will start to make our plans to spread the word to the people of the world to get prepared and to be aware of the evil below us."

"Yes," said Milicent. "It is our responsibility, no matter how hard it may be."

"Yes," echoed Jude, "we must do the right thing and fight against the evil ones."

"Remember what the king said: remember him and he will remember us, and that he is always near."

They hugged each other and said, "Good night," and gave thanks to the king for saving them from the evil and sending them back to help save the world.

The End

CPSIA information can be obtained
at www.ICGtesting.com
Printed in the USA
BVHW092338281221
625046BV00008B/714